WATER

OR GOO

A TANIA ABBEY ADVENTURE

WATER OR GOO

Penny Reeve

CF4·K

© Copyright 2008 Penny Reeve
ISBN 978-1-84550-341-3
Published by
Christian Focus Publications
Geanies House, Fearn, Tain, Ross-shire,
IV20 1TW, Scotland, U.K.
www.christianfocus.com
email: info@christianfocus.com

Cover design Daniel van Straaten
Illustrations by Fred Apps
Printed and bound in Denmark
by Nørhaven Paperback A/S

Mixed Sources
Product group from well-managed
forests, controlled sources and
recycled wood or fiber
www.fsc.org Cert no. 002-296-000
© 1996 Forest Stewardship Council
FSC

Contents

Tania Abbey and Friends

Tania

Daniel

Megan

Tania's Parents

Sam and Emily

Ms Flinders

Mr Campbell

Shanti

MS FLINDERS' BROCHURE

Tania concluded her debate speech with style. "Australia is in drought," she explained. "The dams are almost empty. But each time we turn off the tap, or take a shorter shower, we save water. The future starts with us!" Tania sat down in triumph. She pulled the elastic from her ponytail and let her brown hair flop onto her shoulders. There was no way their team would lose this debate! The class applauded. Ms Flinders, their teacher, stood and clapped her ringed fingers.

"Well done to both teams!" Ms Flinders said, but she looked mainly at Tania. "Your arguments

were clear and well prepared. I will work on the scores during break time, but for now," she checked the clock on the wall, "you can all have an early break. Off you go, but don't make too much noise in the hallway."

Tania let most of the class thunder 'quietly' out of the room until there was just her, Emily and Ms Flinders left. The two girls helped put the debate chairs back under their proper desks.

Tania loved debating. She was good at it. Ms Flinders said that she had 'real potential to change the world'. Tania liked that as well.

"You did good," Emily helped with the last chair. "Shaun almost shot your team down, but when you stood up, they didn't have a hope."

Tania grinned, "Thanks."

"Tania," Ms Flinders called from where she was tidying her totally messy desk. "I received some brochures the other day in the mail, perhaps you would like one?"

She held a leaflet out for Tania. It wasn't really a brochure; it was more like a photocopied advertisement. The smudgy photo showed a crowd of people walking down a city street carrying placards that read "Water is Life," and "Water for the World". It looked sort of like the recycled fashion parade she, Daniel, Sam and Emily had organized a few months ago... only several hundred times bigger.

"What is it?" Tania asked.

"It is the annual Water for the World march taking place this weekend. Did you know that there are over one billion people on earth without safe water to drink?"

Tania scanned the details on the ad.

Date: Saturday 14th.

March starts: corner of Park and Central Street. 10:30 am.

Advocacy Stalls: from 9:30.

"What do you think?" Ms Flinders quizzed. She was always saying that what you said had to match with what you did.

"I'll be there," Tania said. She handed the leaflet back.

"Oh, no, you keep that one. I have a pile to hand out at the staff lunch!" Ms Flinders laughed.

Tania followed Emily down to the seats under the gum trees. The oval was empty and the school quiet while the rest of the classes waited for the bell.

"Are you really going into the city to march with all those people like Ms Flinders?" Emily asked doubtfully.

"Why not?" Tania pushed the straw into her juice. "Do you remember how Ms Flinders congratulated us when she heard we bought those goats for the villagers in India? Imagine what she'd say when we turn up at the Water for the World march. We might even get an award from the Principal, you know, one of those 'Contributing to Society' awards that come with a cheque."

"I don't think my mum would let me go," Emily interrupted. She tugged open her packet of crisps. "And..." she popped a crisp into her mouth, "I don't think your mum will let you either."

WHAT MUM SAID

Tania just stared. Mum continued peeling the carrots for dinner.

"What do you mean, 'No'?" Tania stumbled over her words. She was sure Mum would say yes.

So sure she had convinced twelve other kids from both her class and 5W to ask for brochures from Ms Flinders.

So sure she had run home and chosen the most water-looking shirt and laid it out on her bed with a spare backpack and water bottle – even if the march wasn't till the weekend.

"I just don't think it's a good idea." Mum put the potato peeler on the bench and tossed the last carrot into the pot. "Show me the brochure."

Tania raced back to her room and grabbed the leaflet from the bed. Mum would have to agree it was a good cause, and even if she didn't, surely she knew how important it was for Tania to attend. Ms Flinders was counting on her being there.

Mum read the leaflet, one eyebrow raised and her lips pressed together.

"Tania," she said when she was finished, "why do you want to go on this march? Really. Why?"

Tania glanced down at her stripy socks. "I told Ms Flinders I was going to go... And it is a good cause. Don't you know that millions of people die everyday because they don't get enough to drink? Just think of all the people in the desert!"

Mum's other eyebrow raised. "The march isn't about people in the desert, Tania." Mum stared

at her until she felt her shoulders cramp. "How badly do you want to go?"

Tania jumped on the spot, "Mum, I really want to go. I've told everyone, and I've even packed my bag already," she paused, that bit wasn't exactly true. "But can I please go… please Mum? Pleeeaasse…."

Mum rubbed her forehead. "I will have to talk to Dad about this one. There will be hundreds, maybe thousands of people at a march like this. It's nothing like the fashion parade you did with Sam and Emily; this is much bigger and more serious. But," she placed the leaflet in the middle of the dining table, "it's one thing to do a good deed because you believe in it. It's something totally different to do it because you want other people to be impressed. Even if the other person is someone as nice as Ms Flinders."

Tania slouched back to her room and flopped on the part of her bed that wasn't full of backpack and shirt and water bottle. From the room next door she could hear Megan's music playing. Megan was always playing music. Always reading books or hanging out with her friends. What did she do that was good for the earth? Who ever looked at her and said "Wow, that Megan Abbey has the potential to change the world"?

Tania dropped her head into her hands. What would she say to the kids at school when they found out her Mum and Dad weren't going to let her go to the march? What would she say to Ms Flinders?

Megan turned her music up louder. The lyrics seemed to burn through the walls. "What will you do? What will you say? Who will see Jesus in your everyday?" Tania dragged her backpack up over her head to block out the sound.

THE DECISION

Mum's voice carried down the hall. "Tania, Daniel, dinner!" Tania flicked her maths book closed and pushed her chair back from the desk. She had heard Dad come home fifteen minutes ago and from the smells that wafted into her room, dinner had been ready for a while. But Mum and Dad were talking. Probably about how she was too little to go to the march.

Dinner was already on the table when Tania arrived. Carrots, beans, mashed potato and some strange mince stew stuff that mum called "no shepherd, no pie." The Water for the World leaflet was not visible. Tania sank into her chair just as spiky-haired Daniel bounded up the stairs from the rumpus room.

"I was almost there... so close... Mammoth 14 is really hard, have you tried it yet, Dad?"

Mum interrupted, before Dad could answer, to thank God for the meal. Then they ate. No one said anything about the march. Daniel and Dad were discussing Mammoth moves and tactics. Megan slid her mince around her plate as if in a dream. Probably a dream about boys. World changing stuff, that!

Tania cleared her plate and sat back to wait for the decision. She knew what it would be like: Mum would sit with her arms folded. Dad would do the talking and the answer would be the same as this afternoon's. Tania would have to nod her head to say she understood then come up with a lame excuse to give the kids at school... and Ms Flinders.

Dad cleared his throat, "Mum says you're interested in joining the Water for the World march on the weekend," he said.

Tania looked up, this didn't sound like a lecture.

"Well, Mum and I discussed it and we feel

Water for the World is a good cause and worth standing up for."

Tania couldn't believe what he was saying. She glanced at Mum – she still had her arms folded.

Dad continued, "The brochure you have says that interested people can apply to hold a stall at the City Park after the march. So Mum and I decided that if you can come up with an idea for a stall, an advocacy stall not a cake stall, then we will all go to the march."

"All of us?" Daniel sat upright, "To a march in the city? With posters and skeleton costumes and loudspeakers? Ooooh yes!"

Megan made one of her, 'you're a weirdo' faces. "That was an anti war protest, Daniel. This is about water for everyone in the world, no one is going to wear skeleton costumes."

Dad looked straight at Tania, "Do you understand what I have said to you?"

Tania wriggled in her chair, "I think so. If I can make a good stall idea to hold at the end of the march then I will be allowed to go, and you will all come as well, even Megan."

"If she likes, we won't force her to come if she

doesn't want to. Marches are not supposed to be about forcing people."

"And my stall? I can do anything I like?"

"It has to be something about the Water for the World campaign, something that educates people about the issue," Dad said.

"Something that proves to us you know what you are marching for and believe in the cause more than impressing your friends and Ms Flinders," added Mum.

"I wasn't doing it…" Tania started to say, but she stopped.

"I will email the organisers tonight for a stall application," Dad said, "but I'll need to know your ideas by Thursday night. Understood?"

Tania nodded. This was going to be really big. This was world changing stuff. Ms Flinders would be so impressed.

"Understood."

DO NOT GROSS ME OUT

M s Flinders was not in class the next day, so Tania impressed Emily instead.

"Are you really allowed to march with all those people?" Emily asked during break time. The two of them sat at the top of the climbing frame.

Tania swung her legs, "All I have to do is think of a stall idea; something to educate people about the issue." Tania lowered herself backwards until she was hanging upside down. Emily swung down beside her.

"Can I help?" she asked. Her two blonde plaits

dangled like bull horns from her head. Tania got the giggles. She fumbled for a grip on the bar above and then dropped to the sand below.

"You shouldn't make me laugh when I'm hanging upside down!" she cried.

Emily landed next to her in the sand. "You shouldn't have serious conversations upside down!" She tugged the end of one of her plaits. "Do you have any ideas for a stall yet?"

Tania finished dusting the sand from her knees, "I read the leaflet Ms Flinders gave

me and it says stuff about millions of people dying from water-borne diseases. Do you know anything about that?"

Emily shrugged, "I know in some places if you didn't drink boiled water you would get the runs."

"The what?"

"The runs, you know; diarrhoea, sloppy poos..."

"Oh, you are gross!" Tania stalked away leaving Emily in the sandpit.

"You asked!" Emily ran to catch up. "You can come over to my place this afternoon and we can work on ideas for the stall, if you like."

Tania paused, "Will you tell me any more gross stories?"

Emily walked ahead this time, "Like I said: you asked."

After school, and after Tania had dumped her bag at home, the girls walked down Bracken Road to where the street bent to a dead end. The Georges were renting the house on the corner. It was an old house with five huge gum trees in the front yard that dropped leaves and pieces of bark over the driveway. Tania and Emily strode into the kitchen to find Daniel and Sam perched on the breakfast stools.

"What are you doing here?" Tania asked her younger brother, "I thought you were going to show Sam your attempts at Level 14."

"Yeah, I was," Daniel said. He took the cap off his head and spun it. "But Sam said that Emily said that you were coming over here to work on your stall idea. So we thought we would come and help."

Tania groaned.

They settled themselves in the lounge room. Mr George was working in his study, and Mrs George was in the back yard.

"So, what are we going to do?" Sam asked.

Emily unrolled a large piece of card and handed Tania a felt tip pen. "We can brainstorm, like Ms Flinders gets us to do before we plan our debates."

Tania nodded, then scrunched her nose up. Emily had given her a pink pen. Pink!

"Here, let me have the blue... um...blue for water...," Tania swapped pens. She wrote 'W... A...T...E...R...' in large bubble letters in the middle of the page. "Ideas, anyone?"

"What about hiring a water-slide for people to go down after they do the march?" Sam suggested. Tania let Emily write that one down.

"We could have one of those things that people write their names on and send it to the government," Daniel said. "What are they called?"

"Petitions," said Emily.

"But what would that do?" Sam asked.

"If there are lots of people who agree that water is important the government will be more likely to do something about it," Emily wrote the idea down.

Tania sat back on her heels and let the others talk. Above the bookshelf was a picture of Emily and Sam swimming in a muddy river with Shanti and her brothers. Tania stared at the picture. A funny hesitant feeling grew in Tania's mind. It was the same feeling she had when she was finishing her recycled diver outfit - but before Megan gave her the string of pearls. And the way she felt when the debating team had prepared their argument but something punchy was missing.

She also had the feeling that she had drunk too much from her water bottle on the way home! Trying to hide her red face she ducked out of the lounge room.

Tania found her way down the Georges' wide hallway and past Emily's bright pink bedroom.

The house smelled a bit like an old dishcloth, damp and slightly stinky. The toilet door was at the end of the hall. It was closed so she knocked then pushed it open. Tania screwed up her nose. The tiles on the floor were wet. Didn't Sam know how to use the toilet properly? Maybe it was because in India they had squat-hole-in-the-floor toilets. If she wasn't bursting she wouldn't have bothered. She stepped inside making sure she only stood on the dry patches and closed the door.

But when she flushed the toilet she immediately regretted pretty much everything she had done that day.

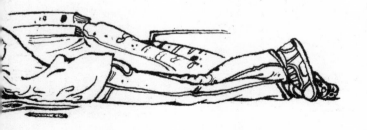

THE TOILET DISASTER

She regretted talking to Emily about the stall because that meant Emily had invited her over.

She regretted eating the packet of crisps for lunch because that had made her thirsty. She regretted not thinking she could hold till she got home because now she had pressed the flush a second time and it was horrible!

In terrible slow motion Tania watched the toilet bowl fill up, all the way to the top. The piece of toilet paper balanced on the rim for just a moment before the water pushed it over onto the floor. In panic Tania pulled at the flush button trying to make it stop but the water kept coming until there was no dry patch left and the water had started running under the door to the carpet outside.

Tania threw the door open in horror. Toilet water was turning the light brown carpet to dark brown. She stepped over it and across to the bathroom to wash her hands. Gingerly turning on the tap she tried to frame words of explanation to Emily's parents. Then she rinsed her hands in the sink and turned off the tap. The water sank away, very slowly, down the plug hole, but when she turned around soapy water was rising from the drain in the middle of the bathroom floor!

"Emily!" Tania called, "Emilyyyyyy!"

Emily ran up the hall. Daniel and Sam thudded to a stop and peered over her shoulder. Tania pointed to the rising water without words. Daniel stepped backwards, his eyes on the spreading darkness on the carpet.

"How much wee did you do?!" he asked tugging his hat down harder on his head as if that would stop the water. But there was no stopping it. Tania looked desperately at Emily. The toilet bubbled like a witch's cauldron.

"Muuuuummmm!!!" Emily screeched. She ducked back up the hallway yelling. Tania just stood in horror. She heard Emily shout something about the toilet and about Tania and a piece of toilet paper. Tania could feel her cheeks burning with more than embarrassment before Mrs George, followed by Mr George, came up the hall. Together they looked from Tania to the toilet, to the carpet, to the gooey puddle on the bathroom floor.

PLUMBING UP A MESS

Emily's dad reached down behind the toilet bowl and twisted the main water tap off. Eventually the water spilling over the bowl slowed to a trickle and then a reluctant drip. It was as if the toilet was disappointed it couldn't flood the whole house. Mrs George let out an exhausted sigh then went to get rags to mop up the mess. She took Emily with her while Mr George stood, hands on his hips, and asked Tania how the disaster had happened. Tania's explanation sounded so silly: "I flushed the toilet... and it filled up... so I tried to flush it again... and the water overflowed..."

Mr George mumbled something about it being bound to happen sometime but then sort of forgot Tania was even there. The boys shuffled back down the hall.

When Mrs George returned from the laundry she sent Tania outside. Emily was waiting for her on the back step. She handed Tania an icy-pole and led the way to the big rock at the back of the

property, right where the back yard turned into the bush of Bracken Gully Reserve.

"Are your Mum and Dad really mad?" Tania asked once they had seated themselves on the rock. Emily shook her head, "I don't think so, the toilet's been leaking for a few weeks, just around the base, nothing disgusting or anything... not like in India."

Tania didn't admit she had thought the wetness was Sam's fault.

"What was it like in India?"

"Like that, but worse. The toilet inside barely flushed so we were only allowed to use it to pee in. For the other stuff," Emily blushed a little "we had to use the toilet out the back."

"You had two toilets? I thought people were poor in India."

"Some are, but we had a good house with two toilets. Shanti's family didn't have a toilet."

"Gross. What did they do?"

"Some of the guys from Dad's office helped them dig a deep pit toilet. They put some walls around it, and a roof and cover to keep the flies out."

"But what did they do before the toilet was built?"

"They used to go in the drain… but the drain was running into the village pond."

Tania waited, she didn't quite understand. Emily went on, "The pond was where the people used to collect their drinking water from."

"Ohh…" Tania let the information sink in. Now that was really gross!

They sat without talking for a while, Emily

sucking noisily at her icy-pole, until the boys started charging down from the house with on-going reports.

"The plumber arrived!" Daniel called. "His truck has a cool picture of Tania's toilet disaster on the side!"

She flicked a twig at his cap.

"The plumber has a huge diggy-sucky-outy machine that he wants to stick down the toilet drain, but the drain is under the house so Dad has to find the torch," Sam ran down next.

"The diggy-sucky-outy machine got mega blocked and the plumber is swearing his head off!" Daniel reported five minutes later.

Back and forth they ran until they crashed onto the grass by the big rock, panting in delight. "We're staying at their place tonight Em," Sam announced.

Tania glanced up at the house. Mr and Mrs George were standing on the back porch talking with the plumber who was writing things on a small pad of paper. Eventually they shook hands and Mr George led the man inside again. Soon they heard the plumber's truck pull out of the driveway.

"What's happened?" Tania asked in a whisper.

"The whole sewage and water system is totally wrecked. It's completely blocked. And I thought things like this didn't happen in Australia!" Sam lay back and laughed in triumph.

Tania felt herself get all hot again. "Why are you laughing?" she demanded. "How can this be a good thing?! You haven't got a toilet anymore! You can't even have a shower or a bath or wash

the dishes! This is going to cost heaps of money to fix… how can you just lie there and laugh like a stupid nong?"

Sam looked up startled, "I just think it's funny," he said, the freckles on his forehead scrunching up.

"Well, it's NOT!" Tania stormed off the rock.

DRINKING WATER

Mrs George was in the kitchen when Tania walked into the house. She was running water from the sink tap into saucepans, casserole dishes, ice cream containers and jugs.

"I'm really sorry, Mrs George," Tania said.

Mrs George pushed a smile onto her face, "Don't worry about it, Tania. It wasn't your fault. The plumber said he is surprised we didn't have a disaster before this. The system is so blocked with tree roots, and who knows what else, it was a disaster waiting to happen. It's a good thing we're used to conserving water from our time in India."

Mrs George carried the pots one by one to the kitchen bench where she covered them.

"Come, I'll show you something."

Tania followed her down the hall. Even under layers of towels the carpet was soggy.

"See this?" Mrs George lifted a large aluminium pot from the hall cupboard. It was shaped like a huge vase, fat at the bottom, then narrow, then wide again at the top. It was about the height of Tania's knees.

"This is a water container I bought in India. Most of the people around where we lived didn't have water taps in their houses. I would watch all my neighbours walk past our house and down to the pond to collect their drinking water. They made at least eight trips with one of these pots, filling it up and emptying it again."

"But Emily said the pond was where the sewage drains went."

"Yes, that's right. There were a lot of sick children in that village."

Mrs George passed the huge pot to Tania. "Perhaps you and Emily could help me? We need to collect as much drinking water as we can before the plumber comes back and turns the water off again."

Tania and Emily filled the pot up at the outside tap. When it was full it was so heavy they could barely lift it, even with both of them holding it.

"The ladies in India carry pots like these eight times every day?" Tania puffed as they reached the back door.

"Shanti used to carry it sometimes if her mum was working."

"Like this?"

Emily shook her head. She leant down and grabbed the pot around the neck, then with a grunt and a wobble she hefted the pot onto her hip.

"Like this," she dropped the pot down again, letting some of the precious water spill onto the back step.

Later, Tania and Daniel waited for Sam and Emily to collect their overnight things then they all marched up the road to the Abbey house.

"Imagine a Mammoth Robot level full of overflowing toilets?" Daniel dreamed.

"Exploding toilets!" Sam suggested.

"Exploding toilets full of toxic waste!" Daniel and Sam ran up the street ducking right and left as if they were dodging life-threatening toilets. The girls followed without the Mammoth moves. Sticking out of Emily's backpack was the roll of card they had started their brainstorming for the water stall on. But the whole toilet episode, and sitting all afternoon wondering if she was going to be in BIG trouble, had snuffed out Tania's enthusiasm for the water march. Not that she didn't want to go, it just didn't seem that important anymore. Even Daniel seemed to have lost his excitement for the idea. The last thing she had heard him discussing with Sam was the best way to put white paint on black fabric – nothing to do with Water for the World at all.

That night the two girls lay in bed, Tania on her bed and Emily on a mattress on the floor. They listened to the boys getting in trouble for talking again. Tania looked at the ceiling. A strip of light from the street split the room in two. Her side and Emily's side. They were very

different. Even in bed Emily wore pink! And now her house didn't have water, just for a night, the plumber had promised. But what if it was longer than that? What would it be like to never have a water tap and have to collect water everyday like Shanti's family did? What would it be like to have to drink dirty water because that was all there was? Maybe that was what the Water for the World march was all about! Tania's mind ran ahead.

Emily whispered goodnight then rolled over, wriggled and rolled over again. Tania stared at the line on the ceiling until she was sure Emily had fallen asleep.

"God?" She spoke the words in her mind. "Please help the plumber fix the mess at Emily's house. And look after Shanti. Help her to find clean water to drink, and a tap near her house so she doesn't have to carry her water pot too far." She lay still as the line of light on the ceiling grew bright, moved a little, then went dull again as a car drove past. Then she whispered, "And Lord? If you want me to go to the water march please help me think of a good idea for the stall…"

THE IDEA

Tania woke up the next morning to see the backwards colours of her curtains on the walls of her room. Emily's mattress was empty, her pink pjs folded up on her pillow. Tania sat bolt upright and slapped her face to make herself wake up. She had a feeling there was an idea just around the corner of her mind. Like the idea had almost come out, but she had woken too soon... or too late.

"Tania!" Mum was calling down the hall. "Get up now or you will be late for school!"

Mum must have called several times already to be using that tone of voice. Tania pushed the sheets back, dumped her pjs on the floor and pulled on her school uniform.

School. Think school…

She ran to the bathroom, dodging Sam on his way out. He had just wet his hair and styled it like one of the famous football players. He looked a little sheepish as he carried his hair brush and a paintbrush away from the bathroom sink. Paintbrush? Tania didn't comment. She brushed her teeth noticing a rim of white paint in the sink, and then dashed to the kitchen. A bowl of soggy wheat biscuits sat waiting for her. That and a glass of plain milk. She shovelled two mouthfuls in and then paused. Her chewing slowed, the swallowing stopped. Spread out on the table was the piece of card from yesterday with the big letters W…A…T…E…R printed in the middle. All around it Sam, Daniel, Emily and even Megan judging by the handwriting, had filled the paper with ideas. Heaps of ideas. Some ridiculous; like a starving people lookalike competition (that must have been Daniel) and some sensible. But it wasn't the ideas that made Tania stop chewing.

Holding the piece of cardboard flat was a vase

of flowers Dad had bought Mum last week. The flowers were old and needed replacing, but not as much as the water they were sitting in. The water was disgusting. It went from sludgy brown at the bottom to yellow green in the middle and to brown green at the top. Filthy slimy stinky water. What if that was all you had to drink? What if...? The idea suddenly ducked out of the corner of Tania's mind. She left her breakfast and rummaged through the kitchen cupboards till she found Megan's old lunch box and a clear glass water jug. She tossed the dying flowers out and poured the gooey water into the lunch box. She only just managed to shove the lid on

tight before Mum came back to the room. Tania gulped down her milk and scooped up the last of her wheat biscuits.

"Where's Emily?" she asked around a mouthful of mush.

"She forgot her schoolbag so had to run home to get it."

Tania swallowed and dumped her plate in the sink. She took Megan's lunch box and the water jug quietly to her room and pushed them under her bed. Then, grabbing her backpack, she ran to the telephone.

"Hello? Mrs George? Yeah, it's Tania," she tried to speak slowly. "Do you think you will need that big aluminium pot by the weekend?... Yeah, the one Emily and I filled up yesterday for you? ... Well, I was just wondering if I could borrow that for a stall I am going to do at the Water for the World march?" Tania pulled a pair of socks from the laundry basket as she spoke and tugged them on. It was quite tricky one-handed. Eventually Emily's mum gave her answer.

"Oh, thank you, Mrs George! Thank you. Tell Emily I will see her at school. Tell her I have an idea for the march."

FILLING OUT THE FORM

Tania's Dad sat at the kitchen table that evening. Looking straight at his daughter he said "O.K. What's it going to be?"

Tania pulled her chair up. "Well…"

"Pleeeaaase say we can all wear skeleton outfits…" Daniel poked his head up the stairs from where he had been playing in the rumpus room.

Tania frowned at him. It was night time and he still had his cap on! She started again, "Well I thought about it…"

"Has Tania come up with a stall idea yet? I

have to tell Marci if I am going to her party or not." Megan leant through the door; she had the telephone pressed to her shoulder.

"If you'll all stop interrupting I'd be able to say!" Tania exclaimed in frustration. "We are going to hold a water stall."

Everyone waited.

"A water stall. Everyone will be exhausted from the march, I've been listening to the weather and it's going to be really hot, so they will need a glass of water. And that's the whole point!" She sat back triumphantly.

Daniel stopped swinging from the stair railing, "what point?"

"The march isn't about people in the desert; it's about how everyone in the world should be able to drink clean water. Dirty water makes people sick."

"I don't get it," Daniel frowned.

Megan moved the phone to her other shoulder, "Hurry up."

"The rich always have clean water," Tania explained, "but what about the poor? Who looks after them? I looked on the internet and learnt that about two million kids die each year because of water and cleanliness issues. That's a lot of kids. "

"Come on... are we going or not?" Megan pushed.

Mum smiled at Tania, "We're going."

Megan sighed and disappeared to her phone conversation but Tania stared at Mum. "I haven't even told you my idea yet."

"I know, but I also know you are now not going on that march just to impress Ms Flinders. You obviously feel the pain of the poor, for that reason alone I would be proud if you, I mean we, marched."

Tania felt her face pull upwards in a huge grin. Daniel let go of the railing and whooped down the stairs and back up again, "I've got to call Sam!"

Dad pulled the pen from his pocket, "So," he started filling out the form. "Tania Abbey, from

25 Bracken Road, phone number 02 4.. 7..."
he started mumbling, "will hold a... stall." He
looked up at Tania, "Will you be selling things?"

"No... well... not really."

Dad raised his eyebrows. He went back to the
form, "How much space will you need?"

"I'll use the trestle table from the garage."

Dad wrote that down.

"And does your stall have a name?"

Tania thought for a moment. The name had
to be something that helped people understand

what the march was about, something that made them think...

"What about..." she paused, "What about: 'Water or Goo'?"

JESUS IN YOUR EVERYDAY

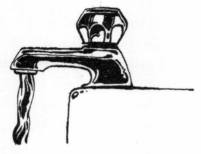

M s Flinders was back at school on Thursday. Her nose was a bit red but she was very smiley and impressed with the amount of grade 5 and 6 kids who were going to the Water for the World march. Each time they told her she raised her eyebrows at Tania as if to say, "Did you do this?"

That night Tania lay on her bed and looked at the ceiling again. She could hear Megan's music coming through the wall, softer this time compared to the other day, but it was the same song. "What will you do? What will you say? Who will see Jesus in your everyday?"

She rolled over and tugged the curtain. The strip of light from outside stretched across the ceiling again. Like the night when Emily had stayed, Tania imagined herself on one side of the line. But instead of Emily being on the other side, Tania imagined Shanti.

Tania had seven water taps in the one house. Shanti's house had none. Tania had two fully flushing toilets. Shanti had a pit toilet dug behind the vegetable patch. Tania had books and toys and clothes that stayed in the cupboard because she never felt like wearing them. Shanti only had two outfits that she wore all the time because they were all she had.

Tania sat up. She flicked the switch to her bedside lamp and pulled over her book of Bible reading notes. She had read something the other day...not yesterday... or the day before... She flicked through the pages until she saw it. The Bible verses were from the fifth chapter of Matthew: "Let your light shine before men, that they may see your good deeds and praise your father in heaven." Tania read the notes next to the Bible verses, "God wants his people to be like Jesus – to love others and stand up for the needy. This verse shows us why we do those things. NOT so other people will see what we do and say how good WE are, but so they will look and say "Wow! Isn't God great!"

Tania flicked the light off. She waited for her eyes to adjust and see the stripe on the ceiling again. She and Shanti were so different, but they were also the same. They were both ten. They both wanted to grow up. The Water for the World march was a good cause. But she had been wrong to think it was about what Ms Flinders or anyone else thought about her.

"Dear God," Tania prayed in a whisper. "I am sorry. Sorry for wanting everyone to think I was great. I don't want this water march to be about making Ms Flinders pleased. I want to please You. I want to go to this march because you care

about whether Shanti gets clean water or not. Because you love her just as much as you love me, and that's what makes you a great God!"

Friday dragged itself by. In the afternoon Tania, Emily, Daniel and Sam made a huge fabric banner in the Abbey garage and then hung it on the clothes line to dry.

"We have finished with the water pot you wanted to borrow," Emily said as she handed Tania the last peg.

"Is the water fixed?"

Emily nodded, making her ponytail dance from side to side. "Mum said that the plumber finished this morning. We have new pipes and two new taps. Now all Dad needs to do is get the carpet cleaned. Are you ready for the march tomorrow?"

Tania watched the banner jiggle in the breeze. "Water or Goo?" it said. What would she do? What would she say? She scooped a small handful of dust from under the clothes-line and tucked it into her pocket.

"Yep, I'm ready."

WATER OR GOO?

Tania leant out the window of their car. "Daniel!" she yelled, "Hurry up!"

Mum and Dad were discussing parking options, Megan was trying to position her legs over the bump on the floor, it was just Daniel's side seat that was empty. Tania looked at her watch. They were already late by eight minutes.

"Come ON, Daniel!"

Dad pressed the horn several times and finally Daniel appeared carrying his grubby old backpack. He bounced into his spot in the car and slammed the door behind him.

"What are you wearing?" Megan asked in horror. "You look like a slob."

Tania eyed the long sleeved shirt and extra baggy tracksuit pants Daniel wore with his ever present cap.

"You do know it is going to be really hot today," she said.

Daniel made a move to get out of the car, "I can always go and get changed…"

"NO!" Tania and Megan and Mum all shouted.

Daniel pulled the car door shut with a grin.

It took over an hour for them to reach the city. Dad found a parking spot near the City Park and helped them unload. They had several boxes of disposable cups, the "Water or Goo?" banner, the trestle table and several bunches of balloons they had bought to attract attention. Daniel started dragging a box of cups up the hill and Tania did the same. Megan and Mum carried the folded table.

Tania reached the stall registration desk first. The woman behind it wore a plain black T-shirt with the slogan 'Water for Everyone' on it.

"Name please?"

"Tania Abbey."

The woman looked over her glasses at Tania.

"Is the stall under your name or your mother's?"

"Mine." Tania tried to look mature and sensible.

The woman made a slight face then scanned the list, "Is your stall called..." she hesitated, "Water or Goo?"

"That's us," Daniel chirped in. The woman took an even longer look at Daniel.

"You are stall number 36. Over near the cypress pine."

They set up the stall where the woman had directed. It was a nice shady spot between two big pine trees. The stall next to it was set up with pens and pieces of paper to collect signatures of people concerned about poverty and water issues. Tania and Megan strung the banner up between the trees while Mum and Daniel unfolded the table below. Mum spread a blue bed sheet over the table and Tania pushed the boxes of cups underneath. Then she arranged the stall's display.

First she pulled out the glass water jug and placed it in the middle of the table. Beside it she left an empty spot for the Indian water pot but filled the rest of the table with empty cups. Tania was glad there wasn't much wind to blow them all away. Then, pleased with everything so far, she found Megan's old lunch box and opened it. The contents had begun to stink like the gunk at the bottom of a blocked drain pipe.

"Yuck!" Megan snatched her hand back and made a face. "That is so disgusting! I thought you had cookies... "

Tania smiled in satisfaction. It was perfect. Slime from the flower vase, a scrap of toilet paper, some oil she had collected from under the car, six pebbles and the handful of dust that she had found near the clothes-line.

"What did you bring that for?"

Tania didn't answer. Making sure she didn't spill any of it on the table she poured the revolting mixture into the water jug filling it right up to the top.

"Now I am really going to be sick," Megan said. "I thought this stall was about giving the thirsty marchers a drink? You can't offer them that!"

"I know. But there is clean water over there," she pointed across the park to where a tap stood beside a drinking fountain.

"Oh look, there's Sam and Emily!" Tania ran over to meet them. Emily was wearing a traditional Indian outfit of long trousers and knee length shirt. It was pink, of course, and on her hip she carried the large aluminium water pot. She handed the pot to Tania.

"Now we're ready!" Tania announced. She carried the pot back to their table and set it proudly beside the jug of goo. But the jug had moved slightly, and there were wet patches on the table. Stranger than that, the jug was now only half full...

WATER FOR THE WORLD

Tania reviewed her last few actions in her mind. She was certain she had filled the jug right up.

"It won't matter much if you only have half a jug of goo, will it?" Megan asked. She was only just beginning to understand the idea behind the stall. "Just fill it up with more water, it will still be gross, I promise."

Tania frowned, but she filled the jug up anyway. Now the stall was ready, although Daniel was no where to be seen so couldn't be counted on to help.

The park was gradually filling up with people waiting for the march but only a few stopped to look at Tania's stall.

"Are you thirsty?" Tania asked them, "Would you like water or goo?" But most of them eyed the jug and pot and then mumbled something about

just having had a coffee and not needing a drink at the moment. By 10:30 Tania was beginning to feel the whole idea was a failure, but then a short siren rang across the park announcing the start of the march.

"Off you go," Dad tapped Tania on the shoulder. "You don't want to miss the start of the march do you?"

"What about the stall?" Tania eyed the crowd gathering by the main intersection.

"I'll mind it. You go and march. But remember our rules: stick with people you know and don't go where it's too tight to move."

Tania wrapped her arms around him for a second then ran across the park. She slipped into the crowd right where Emily and her parents stood. Emily grabbed her hand, "This is so exciting!"

The woman behind the loudspeaker began to announce the direction of the march and then people started moving. Tania gripped Emily's hand. In front of them was Megan and behind were Mr and Mrs George. The crowd spilled off the grass and onto the road. Down the main street they marched, people filling the street. Lots of people wore T-shirts with slogans like the woman on the registration desk. Tania heard others discussing politics and a large meeting where world leaders would be discussing water access for the poor and aid budgets. The woman with the loudspeaker was somewhere up the front of the crowd now so Tania couldn't see her, but she could still hear her.

"All people deserve access to safe clean drinking water," the woman called. "Lifting quality of water lifts quality of life! It is time for our nation's leaders to honour the Millennium Development Goals!"

The crowd cheered in agreement.

Tania didn't shout anything. She just kept marching, wearing her blue T-shirt and hoped, sort of prayed in her heart, that the purpose of this march would ripple as far as Shanti's village.

Tania could barely see her stall when they returned from the march. The day had grown hotter and people milled under the shade of the pine trees and in front of the stall. As she and Emily approached they could hear Dad busy talking and answering questions. He looked almost relieved when they turned up and began answering the questions for him. So far he had not even offered anyone a drink of water. Tania turned to smile at the first 'customer' and swallowed in surprise. It was Mr Campbell.

"Would you like a drink of water, Mr Campbell?" Tania asked. She waved her hand towards the cups on the table, "Water or goo?"

"Oh… um, water… if you have it," he eyed the gooey jug warily.

"We have it, Sir. But it's over there." Tania pointed beyond the group that was gathering. "Over one billion people do not have access to clean drinking water. After I get you a drink perhaps you would like to sign the petition at the next stall?" Then she and Emily lifted the pot from its place and began running across the park. The crowd parted as they ran and they could feel one hundred sets of eyes following them. They placed the pot below the tap and turned it on. Water ran high pitched into the metal until it was half way full. Mr Campbell now stood holding a cup Megan had given him. Emily and Tania, taking one side of the pot each, started jogging, more of a stumble-jog-stagger-stagger-trot, back to the table. They tipped the pot and poured a cup

of cool fresh clean water for Mr Campbell.

He stared at the water for a moment and then tipped it to his mouth. "Thank you," he said. Then he promptly strode towards the petition signing stall.

"I'll have a drink too… of clean stuff, not goo please." Ms Flinders stood in full flowing hippy splendour with her cup held high. "You girls, both of you, are amazing! Let me help!" Ms Flinders put her cup into the hands of a nearby stranger. She lifted the pot and began pouring, cup after

cup for the line of thirsty marchers. When the pot was empty Tania and Emily, or Tania and Megan, or Megan and Mum, or just Dad, ran back to the tap and filled it. Each person that drank went to sign the petition.

AT THE END
OF THE DAY

Tania sank back in the lounge chair. She was exhausted. Megan had gone off to the end of Marci's party. Mum and Dad were still slumped at the dinner table. Daniel had managed to convince Mum and Dad that he should stay overnight at Sam's place, so Tania sat alone in the rumpus room. Her shoulders ached from carrying the water, so did her legs and her arms and her stomach... she even had a little headache that Mum said was probably from spending too much time in the sun. She sat back and closed her eyes

It had been a hectic day. Twice they had run

out of cups and had to send Megan to buy more. They had served teachers, taxi drivers, hippies and business people. Once Tania had poured water into a cup only to find it belonged to a famous cricket player. Dad had wanted the man's autograph, which he had agreed to give only if the stall organiser would sign his cup. So Tania had signed her first autograph, for a famous cricketer! And Ms Flinders had barely left the stall. She helped explain the cause and hand out cups pretty much all day, her smile going from wide to wider. She had even suggested Tania check the evening news because the water march was likely to be on it.

Evening news?

Tania pulled herself out of the chair and lunged for the TV remote. She pushed the power button. The news was on, but it was an article about a new kind of milk for people who don't like milk.

"Is that the news?" Mum called down.

"Yes," Tania called back.

She heard the chairs scrape back and then the slow thud as her parents came downstairs. They sat in the other lounge and Mum leant

her head on Dad's shoulder. But then she sat straight up again. The reporter had changed the topic and was talking about the water march. She listed off the number of people involved and then showed some footage of the crowds and the stalls.

"Hey look, there's Emily!" Tania jumped to the edge of her seat as Emily and Sam ran across the screen with the pot of water. "There's Dad!" Tania almost screamed. The TV crew had caught Dad shaking hands with the cricket player. Tania's head was just visible in the background. And then someone else was on the screen. There was a boy right at the front of the crowd dressed in a black and white skeleton suit.

"Is that...?" Mum gasped.

Tania squinted at the screen. The boy had spiky brown hair poking over the top of his home made skull mask. He was carrying a clear plastic bottle full of Tania's missing goo. A reporter held a microphone to the skull mask.

"If we force people to drink dirty water they will die!" said the boy's familiar voice. "We can help others get clean water to drink!"

Mum sat back in her chair and shook her

head. Dad stood up furious and then sat back down again exhausted.

Tania just laughed. Ms Flinders would be soooo impressed!

EPILOGUE: AT THE START OF THE DAY

Shanti followed her mother along the path toward the village pond. Mother carried the two big aluminium pots, Shanti held the plastic ones. Already the pond was busy. People were washing clothes and washing themselves. One man was washing his buffalo. But the queue for drinking water didn't end beside the sulking animal. It turned up the hill and ended at a concrete block. Out of the block came a tap.

Shanti waited for her turn while her mother discussed a new clinic with the other women. Then they filled their pots with water, hefted one each onto their hips and carried them home again… and again, and again until they had enough water for the day.

Shanti dropped down beside her brothers to catch her breath. They were all healthy these days. God was great. Mother handed her a bowl of water and Shanti gulped it down. Clean water was great too.

You can find the verse about letting your light shine

in Matthew 5:16.

A NOTE FROM THE AUTHOR

When God chose to love us and call us to belong to Him, He sent Jesus to die and be raised up again, and that changed the world. It makes sense then that, as His children, we have "real potential to change the world" no matter how old we are.

Ask God to show you what you can do. What can you learn about? What can you stand up for? What can you pray about? Ask Him, and He will show you.

I'd love to hear how you go,

Penny.

USEFUL ORGANISATIONS

TEAR Australia has a whole lot of kids materials that churches or schools can use called "kids4kids". Go to: www.tearaustralia.org.au

Tearfund UK has similar materials available on its website: www.tearfund.org

They also have a really fun kid's site! Go to www.actionpack.tearfund.org

Always check with your parents before you sign a petition, you might be able to convince them to put their names down also!

CHRISTIAN FOCUS PUBLICATIONS

Christian Focus   Christian Heritage   CF4K   Mentor

Christian Focus Publications publishes books for adults and children under its four main imprints: Christian Focus, CF4K, Mentor and Christian Heritage. Our books reflect that God's word is reliable and Jesus is the way to know him, and live for ever with him.

Our children's publication list includes a Sunday School curriculum that covers pre-school to early teens; puzzle and activity books. We also publish personal and family devotional titles, biographies and inspirational stories that children will love.

If you are looking for quality Bible teaching for children then we have an excellent range of Bible story and age specific theological books.

From pre-school to teenage fiction, we have it covered!

Find us at our web page:
www.christianfocus.com

CF4•K
Because you're never too young to know Jesus